Agnes Lee

The Round Rabbit

Agnes Lee

The Round Rabbit

ISBN/EAN: 9783337185688

Printed in Europe, USA, Canada, Australia, Japan

Cover: Foto ©Andreas Hilbeck / pixelio.de

More available books at **www.hansebooks.com**

THE ROUND RABBIT

The Round Rabbit.

THE
ROUND RABBIT

BY

AGNES LEE

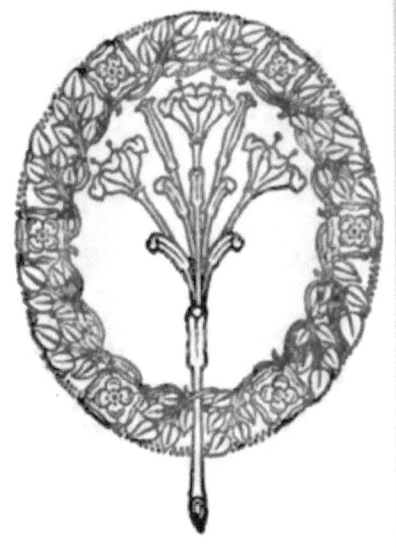

BOSTON
COPELAND AND DAY
1 8 9 8

By the kind permission of the editors several of these verses are reprinted from *St. Nicholas*, *Little Folks*, *Little Men and Women*, *The Chap-Book*, *Babyland*, etc.

CONTENTS

THE ROUND RABBIT

OH, where is my rabbit, my little round
rabbit ?
The flowers tell not, nor the trees.
He had such a sweet, such a queer little habit
Of nibbling about in the breeze.
O, give me my rabbit, my little round rabbit,
To love, and to poke, and to please !

I saw a round robin, a little round robin,
Hop down in the bayberry bend.
I dropped him a bite on the tip of a bobbin ;
But never an ear would he lend,
Though I called : " Little robin, O little round
robin !
Have *you* seen my little round friend ? "

I saw a round stone in the field by the river
I never had seen there before,
A little round stone, yet it made my heart quiver ;
Sad secrets I fancied it bore !
And I flung it afar in the full of the river,
That winced, as I watched from the shore.

Round stone, did you know of my little round
   rabbit,
So soft, and so white, and so dear,
Whose one little pleasure, whose one little habit,
Was loving each soul who came near ?
Oh ! what has become of my little round rabbit ?
I try not to think, nor to fear !

O little round teardrops, away with your winking !
For what gleams so bright down the farm ?
Two small ruby eyes ever nearer me blinking !
Oh something ! oh something ! so warm !
A little round rabbit, a-blinking and winking,
Once more nestles close in my arm !

THE LOST DOG

JOG along, jog!
Out in the fog,
All to be helping a little lost dog.

Up street and down,
Over the town !
Hundreds of houses of russet and brown !

Here comes the rain !
There goes the train !
O to find doggie his home once again !

Weary and wet,
Where shall we get?
Ting-a-ling, dog, let us try it once yet !

Swings a door wide :
Doggie with pride
And never a " thank you " has trotted inside;

Trotted before,
Through his own door,
Bob-tail a-wagging, and homeless no more.

Jog along, jog !
Out in the fog,
All to have favored that little lost dog !

THE TOY BALLOON

WITH my balloon I ran at play,
  And loved the deary so !
But from my hands it slipped away,
And I cried to see it go.

High, high it sailed, and ever so high !
Oh ! I cried as never before —
Till I lost its blue in the blue of the sky ;
And then I cried no more.

For I knew it had touched the curtain thin
That hides the stars and the moon,
And that angel-children had let it in,
And were merry with my balloon.

LITTLE STARS

WHY are the stars so very small,
    Away up in the sky,
And why are lamps so large and tall?
I often wonder why.
And when at eve I lie and rest,
I wonder which I like the best.

I find it very hard to think,
As older fellows do,
That those same tiny stars that blink,
If we walked up — close to —
Would look quite large to little tramps,
Yes, even larger than the lamps.

VANISHED JUNE

OH! have you seen fair June, fair June?
   And whither is she straying?
And is she trysting with the moon?
Or with a star child playing?

The sunshine loved her, and the breeze,
The little breeze that kissed her.
And we who loved her on the leas
Scarce loved her, ere we missed her.

So sweet and happy was her mood,
So gentle was her laughter,
So silent stole she from our wood,
And drew her daisies after!

VANISHED JUNE.

BABY'S MORNING KISS

MAMMA, this morning through the roses'
        bloom,
A lovely angel came into the room.

He took my tiny fingers warm in his,
And smiled on me, and begged me for a kiss.

Oh, he was sweet! and yet I said " No, no,"
And cried — because the angel turned to go.

I called, " I 'll give you one in middle night,
Or I will give you one at candlelight ;

" Or, if you 'll come in one of my short naps
During the sunny daytime, then, perhaps ;

" But do not ask it of me now ; for, ah !
I save my morning kiss for my Mamma !"

SOMETIME

WHEN I ask my father when
We shall leave the town again,
Where the houses hide the sky,
"Sometime," is his one reply.

When my mother, too, I ask
When there'll be no daily task,
And the holidays will be,
"Sometime, dear," she answers me.

Often when the bright days throng
I do long, and long and long
For the sometime to come true,
As it never seems to do.

And I wonder where they are,
Sometime lands, so dim and far;
For to wait I scarce know how!
Oh! is SOMETIME never NOW?

EACH AUGUST DAY

EACH August day
I leave my play,
And comrades blithe and many,
To keep all green
The patch between
The pine-tree and the jenny.

While people pass,
I mow the grass,
Nor heed them in their wending.
I must not gaze ;
For father pays
A penny for my tending.

I play the hose,
Whose water flows
And bathes the lawn in rivers
(Or, now and then
A sleepy hen !
Oh, how she runs, and shivers !)

Nor let it catch
The drying batch
Of clothes upon the jenny
When work is done,
I have my fun,
And spend my father's penny.

THE LITTLE MAN OF MICHIGAN

A LITTLE girl of Michigan
Declares she saw a tiny man,

No larger than the least of mice,
Skating far out upon the ice.

She thought, " How charming it will be
To take that small man home with me.

" I 'll dress him in a coat of blue,
And he shall sleep inside my shoe.

" I 'll put him in my pocket-O,
And take him everywhere I go.

And proud I 'll be, and show with joy
So dear a little living toy ! "

Far o'er the ice she slid, she ran,
To catch her cunning little man.

But as she near and nearer drew,
That little man, he grew, and grew —

Till she, quite close, beheld with awe
The biggest man she ever saw !

And fast her feet they slid, they ran,
Back to the shores of Michigan.

O ROUNDY MOON

O ROUNDY moon above the dune !
This little kindness show me :
To let me rise and through thine eyes
Behold the world below me ;

To let me look on woody nook,
And river smooth and even,
And wander down the silver town,
From hazy heights of heaven !

A–SHOPPING WITH A SHILLING

A–SHOPPING with a shilling on a morning
crisp and fine !
A-shopping with a shilling for that Grandpapa of
mine !

I 'm just a little four-year-girl that likes to skip
and hop,
But I could save a shilling, yes, and spend it at
the shop.

I tried to think what Christmas gift should please
him most of all,
And so, of many things I saw, I chose a little doll.

'T was bought and wrapped and ribboned well
with silken bow-knots three,
And placed upon his table, where he 'd be sure
to see.

And Grandpapa was pleased, indeed, as I stood
looking by.
I knew it ; for I saw the merry twinkle in his eye.

But he is such a busy man, so worked of hand
and head !
"Why she is such a little thing, she 'll need a
nurse," he said.

And I am very happy, for (an honor, you 'll
agree)
Of all the nurses in the town, oh, he has chosen
ME !

12

ROCKING–HORSE RACE.

ROCKING-HORSE RACE

ON, jolly my Rocky!
Your boldest now do!
We'll play there's a jockey
Called Jamie the Blue—

And Tommy the Yellow:
Myself shall be he—
A daring young fellow,
As any may see.

Now fly for your master!
Ah, Jamie has led!
Fast, little mare, faster,
And keep a cool head!

How madly we're racing,
With never a pause,
And is it not bracing
To hear the applause?

On—now we are gaining,
Brave Rocky, my lass,
A thousand eyes straining
To see, as we pass.

Crowds cheering waylay me,
The goalpost outrun.
As there is no Jamie,
I surely have won!

NIMBLEDY-NIMBLE,
  Little Bob Kimball,
Bobby the lively, and Bobby the quick!
Had a great fancy for serving a trick.
Bothersome pranks by the dozen he 'd play.
Mother was calling the whole livelong day :

" *Where* is my thimble ?
O *Bobby* Kimball !
Where are my rings gone? Oh, where is my
  spool ?
Bob ! leave your hiding, and run off to school.
Who left the cellar door open for tramps ?
Who sucked the mucilage off of my stamps ? ''

Once he went maying.
While he was straying
He saw a brown bird sitting under a tree.
He 'd no wish to harm it — just thought he would
  see
How near his stone came to a hit — that was all.
But off flew the bird, and sang down from a
  wall :

" Nimbledy-nimble,
Little Bob Kimball !
Your way of nimble is not the best way.
Little Bob Kimball, O try for a day
NIMBLE FOR GOOD ! and not NIMBLE FOR ILL.''
Said Bob, " Little bird, I don't know but I will ! ''

14

Bobby, he tried it.
As he applied it,
More sweet and more kindly his little heart grew,
Till he was a comfort to all whom he knew.
And now he is welcome wherever he goes;
A fine, merry fellow, as every one knows.
Nimbledy-nimble,
Little Bob Kimball.

FIVE LITTLE POPPIES

FIVE little poppies opened their eyes
One bright May dawn to see the sun rise.
And as they looked, they said, each one,
" O how I would like to be the sun !
For it rides around the world all day,
While we stand still in the field," said they.

Five poppies watched the sun until
It faded and sank behind the hill,
And they said : " After such a long trip about,
The poor old sun must be all tired out ! "
And they drooped their heads in the grasses
  deep,
And five little poppies fell fast asleep.

UNDER PEGGY'S WINDOW

PEGGY

WELL, little violet,
  With starry dews all wet,
A-bloom beneath my window! is this reason?
Why, it's neither May nor June,
And you've really come too soon.
What brought you here the first of all the season?

THE VIOLET

Ah! Peggy dear, forgive,
And let me near you live,
And take me to your gentle heart, and love me!
'T was early, I presume,
Yet what *could* I do but bloom,
With Peggy and the sunshine up above me?

DOWN the street To-morrow flew
To a little boy she knew.

" Here I am, my dear," said she,
" For I heard you calling me.

" Over many and many a mile
I have come to stop awhile.

" But I 've changed (now, would you guess?)
Both my name, dear, and my dress.

" Newly gowned and newly shawled,
Now To-day is what I 'm called."

Said the boy, as best he might
Striving hard to be polite :

" Thank you very much indeed.
You were good my voice to heed ;

" And I 'm very glad you came,
But you don't look quite the same.

" To be frank, when now we meet
You are not one half so sweet.

" To be frank, I much prefer
Seeing you the way you were."

" Ah, I know ! " To-DAY replied,
As she sadly turned aside :

" That is always just the way !
When I 'm known as YESTERDAY,

" And have changed my garb once more ;
Leaving you beside your door,

" You will wish and wish in vain
That you had me back again."

LITTLE TWO

OH! little One had silver fine.
But never silver gift was mine.
For, don't you know ? Of course you do!
I 'm nobody but little Two !

They gave the keepsakes all to her.
I never had a porringer,
Nor mug, nor even (fancy, do !)
A pap-spoon.   Pity little Two !

Pale Dolly, she was pink and gay
When she was little One's, they say.
And so I sigh — and so would you,
If you were only little Two.

No matter.   I can play and laugh.
I mean to have my way by half,
And show them yet what I can do, —
Although I 'm only little Two !

SEVEN LADS

SEVEN lads with seven pence
Bent their brows with thought intense ;

Bobby, Peter, Paul, and Nick,
Bill, and Sam, and tiny Dick.

Trudged they to the toy shop then,
All these merry little men.

And the trouble ?   Never mind !
For the shopman, he was kind.

And he showed his finest toys
To these seven little boys.

And they handled everything,
Ball and kite and top and sling.

When they 'd stayed an hour or more
Billy shuffled to the door,

And he shouted, "Come on, Paul,
For there 's nothing here at all !

"Come on, Bobby ! Dicky dear,
Come, don't spend your money here !

"Come on, Sammy, Nick, and Pete—
Let 's get something we can EAT !"

And they all departed thence,
Seven lads with seven pence !

RACING WITH THE MOON

WHEN by the river run I will,
The moon peeps up behind the mill,
And with a laugh and merrily
It starts to run a race with me.

The moon it starts to run a race,
And nothing seems to keep its place :
The trees advance with rapid stride
To meet me, and the houses glide.

They glide and pass me silently,
And every window winks its eye.
All glide to greet, at evening gray,
Except the moon, that runs my way.

It runs with me the river past,
And when I hurry, hurries fast;
Or slackens, if I slacken do.
And when I stop, the moon stops, too.

THE CAT AND THE BABY

IT'S in that bundle on the bed,
The new arrival, Downyhead.

To-day at dawn I stole aloft,
And there it lay, so warm, so soft!

And I made bold, at what I saw,
To touch it gently with my paw.

They sent me off disgraced, forlorn,
The saddest pussy ever born.

About the dwelling to and fro
The busy footsteps come and go.

I hear glad voices all about,
There seems some joke; and I'm left out;

For no one heeds my sorry lot —
Forlorn, forsaken and forgot.

And, what seems harder still to bear:
My plate stands empty by the stair.

THE TODDLER

LOOK up the street, look down the street,
From out the flowering moss.
If naught you meet, my toddler sweet,
Then may you go across.

Look up the street, look down the street,
Before you leave the gate ;
If horse's feet the cobbles beat,
Stand very still, and wait !

TIRED

I AM as tired as I can be.
I am too tired to take my tea.
I'll go to bed with never a bite,
And rest me well till broad daylight,
And promise like a wise one then
" I'll never get so tired again ! "

LAND OF THE CLUCKING OX

OH, have you heard of that curious land,
The land of the Clucking Ox?
Its ways are hard to understand,
To judge from Curlylocks.

In a dream she went there, and when she woke
(And Curlylocks was May!)
I could but think, from the way she spoke,
She was glad to get away.

She stood in a barnyard, so she says,
As the creatures all drew near,
And she wondered a bit at their bashful ways,
Till — she suddenly felt quite queer.

For, how it happened nobody knows,
Right there in the noonday sun,
" I found," says May, " I 'd fordot my tlo's,
An' I staid, 'tause I *tould n't* run ! ''

Then from their little weeping guest
They turned their blinking eyes,
And one and all they thus expressed
Their mild, polite surprise :

The dog said, " cock-a-doodle-doo ! "
The rabbit said, " bow-wow ! ''
The pussy-cat said, " to-whit, to-whoo ! "
And the portly pig said, " miaw ! ''

THE LAND OF THE CLUCKING OX.

" Cluck-cluck ! cluck-cluck ! " in censure called   *Land of*
The ox of russet-red,   *the Cluck-*
" Baa ! baa ! " the green old peacock squalled,   *ing Ox*
" Quack ! quack ! " the donkey said.

For this was the Land of the Clucking Ox,
And somehow, I must say,
I have an idea that Curlylocks
Was glad to get away.

THE STROLL–AWAY SUNBEAM

A SUNBEAM blithe, in the early day
  Left its father and strolled away
To find the dark.   But all in vain !
It nestled at bedtime back again.
Drooping and tired and tearful, it cried :
" Father, I 've hunted far and wide;
On earth lay many a gloomy spot ;
Whenever I reached it, lo! 't was not.

" Oh, I have hunted everywhere !
By meadows sweet ; by waters fair :
I asked the breeze ; I hailed the lark ;
But, father, I could not find the dark."
And the father kissed his child, and said :
" Of course you could n't, young sleepy-head !
Why, don't you know ? — why, *everyone*
 knows —
There is no dark where a sunbeam goes! "

MISTRESS CONTRARIA BROWN

HEARD ye of Mistress Contraria Brown?
　　When she was up 't was " Oh, to be down! "
When she was down 't was " Oh, to be up ! "
Give her a kitten, she 'd sigh for a pup.

Countryman Brown, thus plagued of his life,
Determined on curing his contrary wife :
He moved her to Boston, where stockings are
　　blue,
And made her read Sanscrit each morning at two.

He fed her on beans, and he sent her, for play,
Up Bunker Hill Monument twelve times a day,
Without any pity, without any pause,
Till she was contented to be where she was.

THE PLAY WATCH

I HAVE a play watch, I have a play watch,
Deep down in my little pocket.
I love it as Jim loves butterscotch,
Or Polly Prang her locket.

For with never a tic, and never a tac,
And never a skip aheadtime,
It 's never too quick, and it 's never too slack,
And it never mentions bedtime.

MAY'S VALENTINE

"IT'S up we'll get!"
Cried Nurse Jeannette,
"To feel the sun a-warming.
St. Valentine
Will feast and dine,
And bring you something charming."

Then dressed they fast
In ruffles vast
This best of little creatures.
But at the pane
She watched in vain,
And ah, the sorry features!

His laughter done,
The sober sun
Behind a cloud went straying.
A heavy snow
Began to blow;
The boys ran in from playing.

"'T will be here yet,"
Said Nurse Jeannette,
"Perhaps at noon, my deary."
The postman passed,
In snow and blast,
And May's blue eyes were teary.

"It's dark and wet,"
Said Nurse Jeannette,
"St. Valentine is groping,

So May, my dear,
Wipe off that tear,
And don't you give up hoping ! "

When twilight came,
The little dame
Still peeped from out the curtain.
The sleet came pelt !
She was, she felt,
Forgotten now, for certain.

But candleshine
Brought Valentine —
A valentine so rosy !
Nor dreamed the miss
' T would look like this,
Surpassing song or posy.

She jumped for joy:
A baby boy
Lay blinking up to greet her.
A brother ! May,
You darling, say
What valentine were sweeter ?

WATCHING FOR SLEEP

'TIS every night I watch for sleep,
   Midst weary thought of books and sums,
And open wide my mind I keep,
To try to catch him when he comes.

But Sleep's a fellow very sly!
I always miss him, in some way ;
For as at night I watching lie,
The very next I know, it's day !

OLD SONG

WHEN I was a-walking, one day, one day,
I met a small laddie, a-crying away.
"Small lad, and what's the matter?" quoth I;
"Why do you cry, and cry, and cry?"
"Alack!" he sobbed, "I've lost a penny,
And now, alas! I haven't any!"
"Then dry your eyes," quoth I, "nor trouble,
Here are two pennies — I make it double."
The small lad smiled with pleasure plain,
But soon began to cry again.
"What, what!" said I, "and still a-sighing?
Now what's the matter, with all your crying?"
"Alack, alas!" quoth he, quoth he,
"If I hadn't lost one, I'd now have three!"

OLD SONG.

THE HASSOCK

THE hassock was so heavy-O,
   I dropped it plump upon my toe !
I could not lift it ; for, you see,
It was too big for little me.

It was so big and heavy-O !
So heavy-O !   No matter, though ;
For some day, when I 'm old and tall,
The hassock will be light and small.

THE HALF-HOUR CLOCK

"OH dear, oh dear!" cried little Prue,
"The old clock's banished for a new!

"The old with frankness struck the hours,
And never failed, for sun or showers.

"But look, to-day, my lessons done,
I heard it well : THE CLOCK STRUCK ONE !

"'T was half-past twelve, as I could see.
The new clock told a lie to me !

"Again I heard, my play begun,
That single sound : THE CLOCK STRUCK ONE !

"Sir Clock," said I, "I'll not obey,
No matter how much ONE you say.

"I played and played, quite long I played,
And wandered in the garden shade.

"Then such a hungry feeling came,
I knew 't was half-past one. Ah, shame !

"To cheat me of my broth and bun,
Yet through the door THAT CLOCK STRUCK ONE !

"A very saucy trick, you know,
To strike three ONES all in a row !"

TOMMY'S ALPHABET

" **N**OW this is A," mamma would say;
   " And this is Q, and this is U,
And this is I.
Now say them — try."
Oh! Tommy was a youngster yet
To learn to say his alphabet;
But, bless his heart! though he was small,
He knew his letters — *nearly* all.
So mother pointed, and her son
Began to name them, one by one.

" This one?" " It's B." " And this?" " It's C."
" And this?"   " It's L; I know it well."
" Nay; try again!"
" It must be N."
" And this one?" — pointing to an I —
" That's you!" was Tommy's quick reply.
Mamma, the error to undo,
Now pointed to the letter U.
Small Tommy pondered; then quoth he,
His face aglow with smiles, " That's me!"

THE children came tripping from out the town,
All in the sunshine mellow.
The children came tripping the dingle down,
And saw a crone in a crinkly gown,
Who, patting a pudding that cost a crown,
Sang, "Jack's a hungry fellow!"

"Your name, O crone, what may it be,
All in the sunshine mellow?"
"My name? My name, it is Crony Cree!
And now, of my name what good have ye?
Come help me all to brew the tea!
Oh, Jack's a hungry fellow!

"Make haste and clear the dingle up,
All in the sunshine mellow,
And gown my cat, and groom my pup,
And mix the meal in the pewter cup.
Jack Frost, my friend, is coming to sup,
And Jack's a hungry fellow!"

"O Crony Cree, our toil hath ceased,
All in the sunshine mellow;
The wind is rising in the East,
The meal is mixed, the pot is greased,
And now we wait to see him feast:
For Jack's a hungry fellow!"

" Nay, get ye back to **town forthright,**
While still the sunshine 's mellow.
He 'll take a nip, he 'll take a bite,
Wherever he can, by dark or light.
Then mind ye make your windows tight ;
For Jack 's a hungry fellow! "

THE NEW UMBRELLA

OH, Ella !
  With her first umbrella !
She walked abroad like any queen.
She held it proudly for display,
Admired its handle, stroked its sheen,
Was ever little girl more gay ?

Dear Ella !
Such a small umbrella !
Once in the rain-swept market-place
I met her; dripping were her curls.
She looked, despite her sunny face,
The most forlorn of little girls.

"Why, Ella!
Where's your new umbrella ?"
Said I; "the storm has drenched your hair !
Just see your frock ! just see your hat !
And what is this you hug with care,
A broom, a fiddle, or a cat ?"

Oh, Ella !
With her first umbrella !
She looked at me and shyly spoke,
The rain-drops pelting on her yet :
"I have it here beneath my cloak,
Because, you see, it might get wet !"

THE CITY GUIDE.

THE CITY GUIDE

WHAT garden 's that ? With pleasure, sir !
   The very garden where
The mad dog ran, that grocer's cur,
That gave us such a scare.

This street ? The prettiest street in town.
Aunt Mary lives on this,
And Baby Prue walks up and down,
And never goes amiss.

The name ? I don't remember ; but
Why need a small girl know ?
I 'm sure it 's where I found the nut,
And lost my bonnet's bow.

I 'm glad I 've helped you, traveller !
No matter what they say,
A city 's very simple, sir,
When once you know the way !

A LITTLE GIRL'S QUESTION

A SWEET-EYED child
Looked down and smiled,
As to her breast
Her doll she pressed,
Then raised her head,
And softly said :
" Mamma, when you
(Before you grew
So tall) wore frocks
Above your knee,
And were, like me,
A girlie small —
Was I your doll ? "

BABY

WHAT is the baby doing, pray,
All the minutes of all the day?
She is too little to talk or creep.
She can do nothing but sleep and sleep.
She cannot read, she cannot sew ;
But she can grow !

What does the little baby soul,
As all the hours strike and roll ?
To it the day is as the night ;
It cannot tell the wrong from right.
It seems to do nothing but slumber so!
But it can grow !

BYE–LOW BILLY

LITTLE Bye-low Billy
Roamed up and down,
Like a white lily,
Through Dreamland Town.

Queer little people
Ran in amaze;
The big church steeple
Stooped down to gaze;

Women stopped knitting,
Each ran to her door;
The birds stopped flitting;
The boats put ashore;

Men stopped working,
And stared, every one;
The cook went a-shirking
The loaves just begun;

The moon fell asunder;
Little drums beat,
To see such a wonder
Toddle down street!

Bill, a bit silly,
Searched in the skies,
Dear Bye-low Billy!
For the sunrise.

Bill, a bit weepy,
To roam, roam, roam,
Said : " I 'm not sleepy,
I think I 'll go home! "

MY FAIR TREE

OH ! my fair tree was my heart's best,
Gowned gaily in the green of spring,
And my fair tree in summer dressed,
The fairest thing !

When down it dashed its veil of gold,
I loved to see it bow and sweep
To autumn.   But at winter's cold,
How I did weep !

Till in the winter, one sweet night,
I saw it white from top to toe,
And through it glancing, light on light,
Great stars aglow !

And now forever choose I do,
As dearest of them all to me,
The little robe that heaven shines through,
For my fair tree.

THE LITTLE HELPER

DEAR cook ! she lets me stir the bowl,
And the sweet flour she lets me roll.

I 'm really helping, while she makes
A fine, rich lot of dainty cakes.

Of all the arts and crafts, now look,
I 'd like to be a kind old cook !

I stir, I pat, I roll away.
Oh ! what a happy sort of play.

But in the oven when they go,
'T is all that I 'm allowed to know.

For little folks may fuss and bake ;
But older people eat the cake !

LULLABY

ROCKING, rocking, bye-low-bye !
Kitty-cat is purring, purring,
And the evening wind is stirring,
Blowing low, blowing high,
While the evening shadows creep.
Rocking, rocking, bye-low-bye !
Sleep, my baby, sleep !

Rocking, rocking, bye-low-bye !
Close thine eyelids, little treasure !
Time another night shall measure.
Little dreams shall hither fly,
Nestling 'neath thy lashes deep.
Sleep, my darling ! bye-low-bye !
Sleep, my baby, sleep !

.

BACK IN BOSTON TOWN

OH ! but it's fine to take a trip
  Along the sunny shore,
To see strange cities past you slip,
You never saw before.

Oh ! but it's fine to see each day
Some new thing of renown ;
To stay a dozen weeks away
From my sweet Boston Town.

Oh ! but it's best to come back home,
To see the Old South spire,
And the distant gleam of the State-House dome,
Like a ball of golden fire.

Oh ! but it's best to be back here
In my play-room, Puss, with you,
Where all the scenes are freshly dear,
And all the old toys new.

THE MOON IN THE POND

DEARLY do I love to linger
In the scented summer air,
And to dip an idle finger
In the pond serene and fair.

There the moon in wide-eyed wonder
Down a mile of azure deep
Slips and shimmers softly under
Clouds most marvellous and steep.

Pebbles light as little kisses
To the water moon I throw,
And in pleasant, cool abysses
Sinking down the sky they go.

FINDING THINGS

I LOVE to roam around,
And look on trees and skies.
Yet sometimes fixed upon the ground
I keep my watchful eyes.

For finding things is fun !
Now have you ever tried ?
One day I found a little bun
With berries baked inside.

And once it was a cent,
And once it was a dime !
A corkscrew very oddly bent
I found, another time.

I found a little toy,
Down where the wild brook sings.
Oh ! am I not a lucky boy,
To find so many things ?

STEPHANA'S RINGS

OH, Stephana's rings were falling
Over her little flannel gown !
They made no jingle as they came down,
Themselves in hush installing.

Oh, Stephana's shears were glancing !
She filled her hands as full as she might,
Spread silken rings on her pillow white.
Oh, Stephana's eyes were dancing !

Oh, Stephana's dreams were creeping,
When we found her shorn on her cloth of gold,
And we smiled and smiled — for who could scold,
When Stephana smiled in sleeping ?

THIS BOOK IS PRINTED BY THE UNIVER-
SITY PRESS CAMBRIDGE MASSACHUSETTS
DURING DECEMBER 1898

www.ingramcontent.com/pod-product-compliance
Lightning Source LLC
Chambersburg PA
CBHW030021030726
47499CB00008B/3070